Bright ≡Summaries.com

The Woman in the Mirror

by Éric-Emmanuel Schmitt

BOOK ANALYSIS

Written by Dominique Coutant-Defer
Translated by Oliver Brown

The Woman in the Mirror

BY ÉRIC-EMMANUEL SCHMITT

ÉRIC-EMMANUEL SCHMITT

FRENCH-BELGIAN WRITER

- **Born in 1960 in Sainte-Foy-lès-Lyon (Auvergne-Rhône-Alpes)**

- **Some of his works:**

  - *The Selfish Sect* (1994), novel

  - *The Other's Share* (2001), novel

  - *Oscar and the Pink Lady* (2002), novel

Éric-Emmanuel Schmitt is one of the most widely read French authors in the world. He lives in Brussels and began his writing career in the theatre with *La Nuit de Valognes* (1991), a variation on the myth of Don Juan, and *Le Visiteur* (1993), a play in which Freud (Austrian doctor, founder of psychoanalysis, 1856-1939) is visited by an enigmatic man who claims to be God himself.

While continuing to write for the theatre, Schmitt also writes novels (*La Part de l'autre*), short stories (*Odette Toulemonde et autres histoires*, 2006) and even an autofiction (*Ma vie avec Mozart*, 2005). Recently, he got behind the camera and adapted two of his works for the cinema, including *Oscar et la Dame rose* (2009).

THE WOMAN IN THE MIRROR

THE STORY OF THREE EXCEPTIONAL WOMEN

- **Genre:** novel

- **Reference edition:** *La Femme au miroir*, Paris, Albin Michel, 2011, 455 p.

- **1st edition:** 2011

- **Themes:** difference, femininity, mirror, destiny, marriage

The Woman in the Mirror features three women in different times and places: Anne lives in Bruges (Belgium) during the Renaissance, Hanna in Vienna (Austria) at the beginning of the 20th century, and Anny in California (USA) today. All three women live in the historical and cultural context of their time, but the same weight seems to weigh on them: that of convention, which they try, each in their own way, to escape.

SUMMARY

ANNE

During the Renaissance, Anne is a rebellious young orphan who lives with the rest of her family – all women – in Bruges. Anne has to marry Philip, but she doesn't want to. So she feels different from her friends, who are attracted to marriage.

On the occasion of her wedding, she was lent a mirror, a rare object at the time, but her jealous cousin Ida broke it, and Anne took advantage of the distraction caused by the incident to flee her wedding and take refuge in the forest, where she spent several days alone, far from everything and completely happy. She has always had a special bond with nature, and it was in contact with it that she experienced her first ecstasies. By running away from her marriage, she feels an intense relief.

Ida and Philippe finally find her and, in anger, tie her up. Then a gigantic stranger, the monk Braindor, appears and puts them on the run. He looks threatening, but is actually very kind: he had supplied Anne with bread during her stay in the forest. After cutting the young woman's ties, he takes her to Bruges and announces to her astonished family that Anne's vocation is probably to become a nun. Indeed, he quickly sensed the young woman's mystical potential.

Later, it is decided that Anne will not marry Philip - to prevent any further flight - but her family refuses to allow her to be religious. At Braindor's instigation, she reads the Bible, which fascinates her, but the violence frightens her to the point of giving her nightmares. She concludes that she is not cut out for the religious life. Feeling called by the wolf that threatens the town, Anne takes part in a hunt and establishes a strange bond with the animal by teaching it to detect traps and providing it with food.

When she returns to Bruges, everyone believes it is a miracle that the wolf has spared her. It no longer attacks the inhabitants. Anne is venerated as a saint and becomes the attraction of the town: "If God had saved this creature, it was because she was pure, a virgin, without sin. (p. 184)

Braindor tries again to convince her of her religious vocation. Happy to escape her family, Anne enters the beguinage - a religious community - in Bruges, but she refuses to join the traditional religion and to read the Bible, which she still finds frightening. She did, however, have mystical experiences when she meditated: mystical poems came to her during her experiences and were collected in her manuscript, *The Mirror of the Invisible*.

Later, Braindor discovers a poem by Anne that confuses him. It was written under a lime tree to which the girl is talking. In it she refers to a higher being in nature, whom she calls 'her lover' (p. 67). The monk claims that this is God. Anne becomes 'a mystical poetess' (p. 295).

Her aunt starts to pay a lot of attention to her, which makes Ida jealous. Ida is also unhappy because she cannot find a husband. In desperation, she sets fire to the family home and is caught in the flames. She survives the fire, but is disfigured by her burns.

Received by the archdeacon, Anne continues to maintain that God is only a word. She lovingly cares for Ida, who attempts suicide after seeing herself in a mirror. Also jealous of Anne's attention to the superior of the beguinage, the dying Ida poisons her and the doctor and accuses her cousin of the murders. Things escalate. Accused of impiety and of indulging in satanic rites with wild animals, Anne is declared a witch and is condemned to be burned alive. She dies peacefully at the stake, in front of the Bruges people, who are angry at this unjust sentence.

HANNA

In 1904, in Vienna, Hanna, who has little interest in marriage, confesses in a letter to her childhood friend, Gretchen, ten years her senior, that she married Franz von Waldberg out of weariness. She finds him attractive, but remains cold in his arms and watches anxiously in her mirror for signs of a possible pregnancy, fearing the disappointment of her family if it fails. She also confides that she is bored in her luxurious home. The young woman is not interested in any of the subjects that directly concern her sex: neither marriage, nor children, nor housekeeping hold her interest, which also adds to her state of perpetual boredom.

After a year of marriage, Hanna relieves her boredom by collecting glassware. She becomes pregnant and finally feels like other women after so much pressure from her peers and in-laws. She hopes that motherhood will fulfill her and allows herself to fall into a "vegetative state" (p. 132), as she believes she has finally found happiness.

Thinking that she would magically bring about her delayed delivery, Hanna breaks one of her glassware pieces. Unfortunately, the doctor tells her that she has had a phantom pregnancy: her belly was in fact full of water. Wishing to clarify the causes of her phantom pregnancy, and on the advice of her Aunt Vivi, Hanna consults a psychoanalyst, Dr. Calgari. She leaves him feeling that she is dealing with a con artist.

However, she decides to go back to the doctor to find out the causes of her obsession with sulphur and the causes of an ecstatic experience of listening to a work by Gustav Mahler (Austrian composer and conductor, 1860-1911): these events help her to understand the value of psychoanalysis. In fact, the psychoanalysis sessions reveal to Hanna her refusal to evolve, her taste for purity and her fear of being a mother. During a hyp-nosis session, she confesses that she was abandoned at birth.

Gradually, she feels attracted to Dr. Calgari, but he pushes her away. She then discovers physical pleasure with a student who was courting her. She then leaves her husband, leaving him his fortune.

In 1912, Hanna became a psychoanalyst in Switzerland and wrote to Gretchen that she had started writing a book on Flemish mysticism after discovering Anne's manuscript *The Mirror of the Invisible* in Bruges. She feels very close to this woman who lived long before her, and she equates Anne's mystical ecstasies with psychic experiences. She has the impression that Anne has written what she herself feels, centuries later.

Two years later, Gretchen writes to Hanna's ex-husband to warn him that Hanna was indeed raised by her real parents, but that she disowned them because they were not aristocrats. They died accidentally shortly afterwards, and Hanna hid her guilt under the fable of abandonment, which poisoned her life. She also recalls Hanna's death in the early days of the First World War (1914-1918).

ANNY

In modern-day Hollywood, Anny, an eccentric 20-year-old actress and cocaine addict, is surprised to be in love with David. One night, to impress him, she indulges in dangerous acrobatics in a nightclub and is crushed by one of the disco balls in which she loves to contemplate herself.

In the hospital, Anny becomes addicted to morphine. Ethan, a nurse, wants to detoxify her, while Johanna, her agent, takes advantage of her accident to advertise, without the slightest concern for her client's condition. During her stay in hospital and her talks with Ethan,

she realises that she is unhappy and unloved. She realises that she thought she loved David, but that she did
not.

Now back on her feet, Anny is able to resume filming.
She checks the thick make-up covering her scars in a
mirror. She is now living with David, a charming and
manipulative man, but she is also happy to see Ethan
again, who does not leave her indifferent. Despite his
obvious attraction to the actress, Ethan refuses her
advances, convinced that she just wants to add him to
her list of conquests before getting rid of him.

Out of spite, Anny has sex with the film's director and
doesn't go on a date Ethan gave her. Overpowering the
director since she became his mistress, the young
woman is temperamental on the set. An old actress,
nicknamed "Sac Vuitton" (p. 214), warns her that she
will lose herself if she continues to lead this exalted life,
but without real pleasures.

Anny agrees with Johanna, who urges her to give up
alcohol and drugs, but she secretly sets herself the goal
of reaching an alcoholic coma in three days. At the
screening of her film, she is finally found unconscious
by Ethan, victim of an overdose.

Johanna turns Anny's rehab into a multi-million dollar
media event, and in the hospital, the actress is constantly stalked by cameras behind one-way mirrors.

Later, Ethan confesses to her that he is on drugs.
Disabling the cameras that film the young woman in

her hospital room, they have sex. The director of the clinic fires Ethan, judging that he is spending too much time with Anny. Having interrupted her treatment, Anny attends the funeral of "Sac Vuitton" and visits Ethan in prison, where he is incarcerated for stealing drugs from the hospital.

Some time later, the reader finds Anny, who has retired to the seaside and found Ethan, who has been released from prison but is still on drugs. She turns down all offers of scripts, except that of a European director who offers her the role of Anne of Bruges in his film. This man is in fact Gretchen's grandson, to whom Hanna had dedicated her book. Anny and Ethan meet him in Paris.

Anny, completely transformed, is making the film about Anne's life in Bruges. At the beguinage, she is mysteriously attracted to the old lime tree to which Hanna had already instinctively gone a century earlier.

CHARACTER STUDY

ANNE

Known as the Virgin of Bruges, Anne lived in this Flemish city during the Renaissance. Orphaned by her mother and unknown father, she left an isolated farm in northern Flanders and moved to Bruges with her family, which consisted mainly of women – grandmother, aunts and cousins.

This beautiful blond teenager refuses to marry young Philippe and constantly takes refuge in nature, with which she has always had an exalted and strange relationship, leading to her first mystical ecstasies. Anne sees life in a way that is different from others, and she stands out in a society where she is expected to fit in with the established norm. She should marry a man from a good family and bear him children, and thus lead a very traditional life, like millions of other Catholic girls in the Renaissance, but Anne longs for freedom and nature; she knows that she cannot find happiness if she is confined to a stereotypical family life.

Retired to a religious community, although rejecting the dogmas of Christianity, she appreciated the simple life of the beguinage, as she felt free from the social constraints (such as marriage) that she sought to escape. She had an original and progressive view of religion for her time, as she challenged the actions of God in the Bible.

Throughout the novel, Anne shows great compassion for her cousin Ida, who has hated her all her life. It is she who schemes to lead the young woman to her doom. In fact, Anne ends up being burned as a witch, accused of heresy and a victim of the accusation of poisoning brought against her by Ida, who has always been jealous of her beauty and success.

HANNA

The chapters on Hanna are epistolary: they are letters she writes to her friend Gretchen over several years. Hanna has just married Franz von Waldberg, a Viennese nobleman, who offers her a lavish life. Hanna did not marry him for love, but because she was tired of her single life. She does not like married life either, and only her glass collection brings her some happiness ('Apart from my collection, nothing about the day ahead appeals to me', p. 96). She has no desire to have children and become a mother, but the stress she feels from the continuous pressure from her surroundings to get pregnant leads to a phantom pregnancy.

Like Anne, Hanna does not fit in with the expectations of a woman of her time: marriage, children and domestic duties are of little interest to her. Although she is old enough to be considered a lady, she feels that she is disguising herself when she dresses as a woman; she remains a 'mere girl lost in the land of women and forced to mimic the adult' (p. 29). Hanna therefore lives a lie, and pretends every day to be a character that does not fit her, in which she does not recognise herself. For example, she accepts sexual relations with her husband only because she thinks it is her role, without even feeling any attraction for him.

The young woman knows that she has everything she needs to be happy, but she is unable to achieve the happiness she so desperately seeks: 'Every day I remind myself that I am posh, loved, desired, housed in a palace, introduced to the best society in Vienna; every hour I force myself to admit that I am in excellent health, that I eat more than I need' (p. 95). To prevent people from taking an interest in her and discovering her deep distress, she prefers to take an interest in them and gather their own confidences.

Her life changes when she discovers psychoanalysis: she finally gets rid of social conventions and leaves her husband to live the independent life she has always dreamed of (in Switzerland, then in Belgium). Psychoanalysis also enabled her to detach herself from her glass collection, which had become an unhealthy obsession.

ANNY

A Hollywood actress in the 2000s, the beautiful and eccentric Anny, aged 20 and born of unknown parents, leads a dissolute life, between drugs, alcohol and antidepressants that accentuate her penchant for self-destruction. As Ethan rightly remarks, she 'runs away from her inner life' (p. 77), refusing to think and panicking whenever she thinks about the future.

Anny accumulates male conquests, to the point where she passes men wondering if she has slept with them, but she is well aware that this does not really satisfy her. She has the nerve to charm a policeman in order to escape a fine. As Tabata, an old actress, remarks, Anny is "not happy because [she] opens [her] door to immense feelings" (p. 222): "When you laugh, you laugh: you don't sneer... When you cry, you cry: you do not whine... Everything in you is great, nothing petty, nothing small." (*ibid.*) Her sensitivity is also expressed in her acting talent, which quickly propelled her to the top of the bill.

A young nurse, Ethan, wants to detoxify her. She falls in love with him, even though he is also a drug addict. She finally gives up her hectic life, goes into exile by the sea and finally finds a role in the movies that really suits her: Anne of Bruges.

As an actress, she is also forced to play a role all the time, sometimes engaging in publicity photo shoots and reluctantly starting an affair with David, a handsome actor, simply because it would be good for her image.

ANNE'S ENTOURAGE

The monk Braindor

This tall and frightening man of the cloth rescues Anne when she first runs away in the forest; he will never stop protecting and advising her. The monk Braindor, aware of the girl's mystical temperament and intrigued by her personality, tries several times to convince her to enter the orders, multiplying theological arguments. His wish was finally granted when Anne entered the beguinage.

Ida

Ida is Anne's cousin and her nappy sister. Deeply jealous of her cousin's marriage, of her beauty, and of the attention she receives from others, she repeatedly provokes and insults her. She goes so far as to set fire to the family home and remains trapped in the flames. Saved by Anne, who watches over her during her convalescence, she reproaches Anne for her affection for the superior of the beguinage. She then poisons the doctor and the mother superior, accusing Anne of these crimes. It is she, again, who accuses Anne of witchcraft and brings about her death.

HANNA'S ENTOURAGE

Aunt Vivi

Considered "the clan's hussy" (p. 60) who collects lovers, she is Hanna's husband's aunt. Her familiarity allows the two women to gradually become friends: Aunt Vivi gives the inexperienced young woman advice on grooming and manners, and also takes an interest in her intimate life. She discovers Hanna's deep imbalance and advises her to undergo psychoanalysis. It is also she who discovers (and keeps quiet), by practising the art of the pendulum, that the young woman is not really pregnant. Hanna admires her for her extreme femininity and her avant-garde stance.

Franz

Franz is Hanna's husband and hat enthusiast. Kind and loving, he is very happy with his marriage and only wants children to complete his happiness. He idolises Hanna ('I am exceedingly lucky to have been chosen by the bewitching Hanna', p. 98), but is blind to her unhappiness and does not realise that she will soon ruin them with her collection of sulphurs. He is not told of Hanna's phantom pregnancy until her death, by Gretchen.

ANNY'S ENTOURAGE

Tabata Kerr, aka Sac Vuitton

"Sac Vuitton" is the nickname of a grandiloquent old Hollywood actress, given to her because of her scarred face from plastic surgery. Now ugly and obese, she uses Anny's celebrity – who worships her – to appear in celebrity magazines. But it is also she who convinces the young actress of her talent and advises her to get back on track.

Ethan

A young nurse who is a drug addict, he takes care of Anny after she falls in a nightclub. He helps her feel better by administering morphine. Once out of the hospital, Anny sneaks out to see him in the evening to get her doses. Ethan is in love with her, but he needs time to admit it to himself. He makes Anny question the reasons for her sexual escapades.

KEYS TO READING

A SPECIFIC NARRATIVE PATTERN

The Woman in the Mirror tells the story of three women living in different places and at different times: the first, Anne, lives in Bruges during the Renaissance; the second, Hanna, in Vienna at the beginning of the 20th century; the third, Anny, in California a century later. Where the reader might have expected a text divided into three successive blocks, each devoted to one of the three characters, the author has chosen to alternate: the novel opens with the presentation of Anne, then the second chapter is devoted to Hanna, and the third is devoted to Anny. The rest of the text follows the same narrative principle, always evoking the three women in the same order.

The novel is thus ordered according to a strict tripartite division, with each woman having the same number of pages in each chapter and the same number of chapters in the book. The continual switching from one woman to another – in a constant shift between Bruges, Vienna and California, on the one hand, and the Renaissance, the 20th century and the 2000s, on the other – gives the story a particular rhythm: the respective plots are regularly interrupted and resumed later.

The three women enter the stage alternately, as if on a theatre stage where they would each play their part in turn, surrounded only by a small number of companions

– the historical context and the places of the action being evoked only if they serve to paint their evolution.

There are few descriptions in *The Woman in the Mirror*, except for the settings in which Anne, Hanna and Anny live: the forest and the beguinage of Bruges, the pleasure spots of the Viennese aristocracy, the trendy nightclubs and the Hollywood film sets. The women's physical appearance is not detailed, the author choosing to give priority to their psychological reactions to events. This aspect is particularly marked in Hanna's story, since it is through her point of view, expressed in her correspondence with her friend Gretchen (whose answers are not known), that the reader becomes aware of the facts of her life and their repercussion in the young woman's mind.

Finally, it is obvious from the beginning of the novel that the author wants to establish a parallel between these three women's destinies – if only by the similarity of their first names – between which the reader very quickly perceives similarities. This intention is explicitly expressed in the last three chapters, towards which the whole text converges: Anny meets a director who wants to direct the story of Anne of Bruges, which was bequeathed to him by his grandmother Gretchen, Hanna's pen pal; finally, the actress, on her way to Bruges to shoot the film, feels mysteriously attracted to the tree under which Anne used to stay four centuries earlier, and under which Hanna had already lingered, then on a tourist visit to the beguinage.

The three main lines of the novel come full circle and become one.

A THREE-FACETED PORTRAIT OF A WOMAN

Together, the three heroines create a three-faceted portrait of a woman. Their respective appearances in time, at three different periods, could evoke metempsychosis, a theory according to which the same soul can animate several human, animal or even vegetable bodies successively. It is as if these three women were one, repeating a destiny centuries apart, through successive reincarnations – all the more so since the title of the novel evokes a single woman.

 ## METEMPSYCHOSIS

From the ancient Greek *metempsúkhôsis*, meaning "displacement of the soul", metempsychosis is the ancient belief that one and the same soul can inhabit several human, animal or vegetable bodies successively. It obviously assumes a duality between the soul and the material body, and leads to the idea of reincarnation, which is still present in some religions today.

Many Greeks explored this idea, including Plato (Greek philosopher, c. 427 BC – c. 348 BC), who believed that whether a human is reasonable or aggressive determines whether he or she will be reincarnated as a gregarious or prey animal, and Pythagoras (Greek mathematician and philosopher, c. 570 BC – 480 BC), who said that he recognised a beaten dog as one of his former friends because of his empathy for the animal.

Closer to home, the term is also present in James Joyce's (Irish writer, 1882-1941) *Ulysses* (1922), where it proves the hero's erudition without being further defined; Marcel Proust (French writer, 1871-1922) includes it on the first page *of In Search of Lost Time* (1913-1927), while Jorge Luis Borges (Argentinian writer, 1899-1986) makes it the subject of his short story *The Approach to Al-Mu'tasim* (1944).

Without necessarily adhering to this thesis, which is never explicitly mentioned by the author, we can nevertheless explore the close links between the three characters. "How much we resemble each other over the centuries" (p. 424), Hanna herself says when she decides to write a book about Anne, whom she calls "her labyrinth sister" (p. 425). The similarities between the three women multiply throughout the book.

A problematic childhood

The three women in the novel have a painful family past in common, whether real or fantasised:

- Anne, who never had a father and whose mother died giving birth to her, was taken in by her uncle and aunt. From then on, she fears that 'she owes her existence to a sacrifice' (p. 117);

- Hanna, after reading a book about Marie Antoinette (Queen of France, 1755-1973) as a child, decided that she wanted to be a queen. She then blamed her parents 'for not having blue blood' (p. 443), declared that she was probably not their real daughter, and invented a more prestigious genealogy. This fable led to many troubles for the young woman;

- Anny did not know her real parents and was raised by a couple with whom she decided to have a good relationship to avoid problems. However, she left them at 16 to pursue her acting career.

A world of women

The three women's entourage is essentially female, whether it has a positive or negative influence on the heroines:

- Anne first lives with her aunt and cousins (including Ida, who hates her), then joins a religious community of women;

- Hanna is under pressure from her husband's many aunts and cousins, and in her letters she pours her heart out to her friend Gretchen;

- Anny receives advice from a returning actress, Sac Vuitton, and professional guidance from her agent, Johanna.

The male characters in the novel, on the other hand, seem a little weak compared to their female counterparts and play secondary roles:

- Anne's young fiancé is quickly ousted, and she resists the monk Braindor's arguments throughout the story;

- Hanna's husband is caring, but without real substance;

- The countless men who gravitate towards Anny appear to be a stopgap. The actress thinks she is falling in love with a handsome man, David, and is then attracted to Ethan, who is unable to free himself from drugs.

The affirmation of a difference

"I feel different," she murmured. (p. 9) The novel begins with this sentence from Anne, as she is being prepared for her wedding to Philip. Similarly, Hanna, who should be overjoyed at the prospect of marrying the handsome and wealthy Franz von Waldberg, confesses that she is doing it 'like testing a remedy' (p. 28). Anny, for her part, feels like a stranger to herself, aware that she is not living the life that is right for her.

All three women feel this painful sense of difference, mainly in relation to what others expect of them: marriage, motherhood, family life. "I don't know how to be the woman that our time demands. I find it hard to be interested in matters of our sex" (p. 29), says Hanna. As for Anny, she aspires to an exceptional destiny and exults when she discovers among the beguines that "one [can] set oneself other goals than sweeping up, undergoing the domination of the male, laying children and wiping them" (p. 293). Finally, Anny is perpetually oscillating between the desire to conform to the model of the rich and adulated actress imposed on her by the Hollywood milieu and the adherence to her deep, solitary and sentimental nature.

It will take the three women a long time to find a way to escape the fate that society has in store for them:

- mysticism and poetry for Anne;

- psychoanalysis and writing for Hanna;

- detoxification and a kind of return to nature for Anny.

In addition, they develop solutions after all three have been victims of various addictions: the impossibility of living anywhere but in nature for Anne, the manic collection of sulphur for Hanna and drugs for Anny.

Should *La Femme au miroir* be seen as a feminist novel? In any case, it appears as a tribute to those women who, at different times, were able to free themselves from the constraints imposed on them, by becoming aware of their deepest nature, always associated with an immoderate taste for nature in general – even if this is revealed late for Anny. Throughout the novel, the heroines assert their difference and their incomprehension of the world around them.

THE MIRROR THEME

The theme of the mirror is frequently used in literature. The mirror plays an important role in many stories: the surface of the water reflecting the image of Narcissus in the *Metamorphoses* (AD 1 or 2) by Ovid (Latin poet, 43 BC-17 or 18 AD).C.), to the mirror in which the Princess of Cleves (novel by Mme de La Fayette [French woman of letters, 1634-1693], written in 1678) notices that the Duke of Nemours is stealing her portrait, the mirror that the stepmother of Snow White (1812) questions in the fairy tale by the brothers Jakob and Wilhelm Grimm (German writers and philologists, 1785-1863 and 1786-1859), or the mirror-painting in the *Portrait of Dorian Gray* (1891) by Oscar Wilde (Irish writer, 1854-1900), etc.

A novel centred on three women's destinies, Éric-Emmanuel Schmitt's story associates women and mirrors in its title, but here the mirror goes beyond its function as an object, which consists of reflecting, more particularly to women, a more or less flattering image of their person – it also fulfils this role in the novel, however, when it reflects back to Ida, Anne's cousin who has been badly burned, the image of her ravaged face, thus driving her to suicide. In fact, the mirror has mainly a symbolic function in the novel. It appears in the first three chapters, devoted to each of the heroines:

- A precious and rare object during the Renaissance, reserved for the nobility, it was lent to Anne on the occasion of her wedding preparations. The object aroused the admiration of those who did not own one. Anne then sees her image for the first time, which is certainly ravishing, but which does not seem to correspond to her ("She was looking at a stranger [...], she did not look like her", p. 12). This episode echoes the first line of the novel, where the girl asserts her difference. Moreover, the precious mirror breaks at the end of the chapter, signifying Anne's break with the destiny she has been given and the impending cancellation of her marriage. This incident serves as a trigger for Anne to 'tear herself away from unhappiness' (p. 46);

- Hanna encloses a portrait of herself with Franz in her first letter to Gretchen. She describes herself as 'a courtly girl with an embarrassed smile' (p. 26) who does not recognise herself under the extravagant hats her husband likes to put on. Her correspondence with her friend also acts as a mirror for her own image. Her existence is in a way duplicated by the way she describes it in her letters. In addition, the young woman's passion for glass and sulphur is to relieve her existential boredom, and she constantly contemplates the reflections and play of light. In fact, it is by breaking one of them that she thinks she can induce, in an almost magical way, her delivery. The birth takes place immediately, revealing the young woman's false pregnancy, as if the glass object had broken all appearances. Years later, the psychoanalysis having borne fruit, she throws her entire expensive collection into the Danube, like so many pretences that she gets rid of;

- Anny is used to contemplating herself in the disco balls of the nightclubs she frequents. "Who is that whore?" (p. 32), she asks herself in the first chapter. The next moment she realises that it is her, but, completely drunk, is amused by it, in the same way that, throughout the story, she hides her malaise by taking various drugs. The theme of the mirror is then recurrent in the story of the young actress, who lives constantly in the world of the image (incessant paparazzi photos, cameras hidden in one-way mirrors to track her without her knowledge, etc.).

The mirror, in all its forms, is thus omnipresent in the novel, constantly sending back to the heroines false or truncated images of themselves, symbols of the existence they lead and which does not correspond to them, images of women as others would like to see them. And it is only when the young women are away from their reflections that they can become themselves again: Anne is immersed in her contemplation of nature; Hanna confesses her most shameful thoughts, and Anny sheds the mask she puts on for the press.

 ## THE MIRROR IN THE ARTS

The mirror is not only a literary motif. From the Renaissance onwards, mirrors played an important role in painting, as they allowed artists to present portraits from new angles: Let us think in particular of the *Arnolfini Husband and Wife* (1434) by Jan Van Eyck (Belgian painter, 1390-1441), where the mirror reveals the painter working on the couple's portrait, whereas he traditionally never appears on his own canvases; or the *Venus with a Mirror* (1650) by Diego Velázquez (Spanish painter, 1599-1660), where Venus, naked, contemplates herself in a mirror held by her son Cupid; or the *Woman with a Mirror* (circa 1515), by Titian (Italian painter, 1488-1576), where two mirrors surround the female figure (one behind her, and one in front of her, so that she can observe her hairstyle from the back)

In cinema, the mirror is often used to convey a stereotype: as in *Woman in the Mirror*, the woman who looks in the mirror often shows her vulnerability; the person she observes in the mirror does not necessarily correspond to the person she presents to the rest of the world, as is the case for Natalie Portman (Israeli-American actress, born in 1981) in the film *Black Swan* (2010)

In Cocteau (French poet, playwright and filmmaker, 1889-1963), the mirror is used to expose an invisible reality, showing the duality between being and appearing: for example, in *Beauty and the Beast* (1946), Belle's sisters see an old lady and a monkey when they look into a mirror. Orson Welles (American filmmaker and actor, 1915-1985) exploits the mirror theme in *The Lady from Shanghai* (1948), where a married couple kill each other in a maze of broken mirrors, in a duel from which only the narrator (played by Welles) emerges unscathed: this scene has become famous and many films have attempted to refer to it, such as *The Third Man* (1949) or *Inception* (2010).

THREE PLACES, THREE ERAS AND THE SAME STRAITJACKET

In his novel, Éric-Emmanuel Schmitt has chosen to place his heroines in three distinct space-time settings. These have obviously not been chosen at random and are linked to the respective destinies of the three young women:

- Bruges and the Renaissance. The city of Bruges is a 'shock' (p. 14) for Anne. She, who previously lived in the country, discovers the city, a world that is completely different from the one she has been used to. Moreover, this move also corresponds to her transition from childhood, an innocent state, to the status of an adolescent, with the problems that this entails, such as marriage. In fact, in this Catholic place and time, all the inhabitants expect Anne to marry and give birth, which she refuses and avoids, although she does discover a certain mysticism;

- Vienna in the early 20th century. The city of Vienna is hardly described in the novel; it is mainly chosen for its connection with Sigmund Freud and the birth of psychoanalysis. This geographical proximity allows Hanna to be one of the first to benefit from this new approach thanks to Dr. Calgari. Her relationship with Vienna is also inseparable from the turmoil of her marriage. After her travels, she lived there for the duration of her marriage to Franz, but once it was over, she fled and settled in Switzerland, leaving both her husband and her place of residence;

- California today. Living in one of Hollywood's jet-setting hot spots, Anny is surrounded by multiple superficial temptations (relationships with strangers, plenty of alcohol, drugs, etc.). As a result, the young actress lives in a permanent state of malaise. When she went to Europe to make the film about Anne of Bruges, she found a simpler world, away from the paparazzi. This new environment allowed her to experience a new form of serenity, which had been alien to her until then.

Despite their striking differences, these three periods and places share commonalities that unite the fate of the three heroines:

- the omnipresence of the gaze of others. Although the secondary characters are only minimally detailed, they play a crucial role, as their gaze influences the actions of the three women. Anne runs away from her marriage because she cannot stand the family pressure to marry. Later she joins the order of nuns, influenced by Braindor's opinion of her faith. The pressure from Hanna's family circle to give her husband an heir is so great that it causes a phantom pregnancy. As for Anny, she is constantly playing a role in front of the cameras, under the impulse of her agent who wants to make as much money as possible;

- the social conventions of the couple that become too strong. Each era has its own social conventions, which the heroines do not want to follow. As a result, they feel immensely different from those around them. Anne rejects marriage to a good party and a life as a wife and mother. Hanna is a wife, but does not find happiness in this situation and is not in the least interested in motherhood. Anny leads a dissolute life where she drowns her unhappiness in drugs, alcohol and sex, never having any desire for a traditional couple relationship.

The three women we meet at the beginning of the novel are locked into a similar straitjacket, despite the different places and times in which they live: they all suffer from their differences, from their non-conformity to the prevailing norms, which leads them to feel very alone. *The Woman in the Mirror* traces their personal journeys to escape from their oppressive circumstances and find happiness and fulfilment.

AVENUES FOR REFLECTION

A FEW QUESTIONS FOR FURTHER REFLECTION...

- How do you understand the title of the work? Interpret it.

- Detail the narrative structure of the novel. How is it original?

- What differences do you notice in Hanna's writing between the time she lives in her illusory world and the time she is liberated by her psychoanalysis?

- What is the relationship between Braindor, Aunt Vivi and Sac Vuitton?

- Although they live in different times and places, what do the three female figures in the story have in common?

- Can *The Woman in the Mirror* be associated with the genre of the psychological novel? Explain.

- What image does the author portray of the male characters in this novel (Braindor, Franz, Ethan, etc.)? How do you explain this?

- Can *La Femme au miroir* be described as a feminist novel? Justify.

- What role does nature play in the novel?

- How do the final chapters explicitly link the fates of the three heroines?

TO GO FURTHER

REFERENCE EDITION

SCHMITT É.-E., *La Femme au miroir*, Paris, Albin Michel, 2011.

Your opinion is important to us!
Leave a comment on the website of your online bookshop
and share your favourites on social networks!

Ebook EAN: 9782808686747
Paperback EAN: 9782808698146
Legal Deposit: D/2023/12603/1094

Cover: © Primento
Digital conception by Primento, the digital partner of publishers.